Cadillac Crew

by Tori Sampson

No one shall make any changes in this title(s) for the purpose of production. No part of this book may be reproduced, stored in a retrieval system, scanned, uploaded, or transmitted in any form, by any means, now known or yet to be invented, including mechanical, electronic, digital, photocopying, recording, videotaping, or otherwise, without the prior written permission of the publisher. No one shall share this title(s), or any part of this title(s), through any social media or file hosting websites.

For all inquiries regarding motion picture, television, online/digital and other media rights, please contact Concord Theatricals Corp.

MUSIC AND THIRD-PARTY MATERIALS USE NOTE

Licensees are solely responsible for obtaining formal written permission from copyright owners to use copyrighted music and/or other copyrighted third-party materials (e.g., artworks, logos) in the performance of this play and are strongly cautioned to do so. If no such permission is obtained by the licensee, then the licensee must use only original music and materials that the licensee owns and controls. Licensees are solely responsible and liable for clearances of all third-party copyrighted materials, including without limitation music, and shall indemnify the copyright owners of the play(s) and their licensing agent, Concord Theatricals Corp., against any costs, expenses, losses and liabilities arising from the use of such copyrighted third-party materials by licensees. For music, please contact the appropriate music licensing authority in your territory for the rights to any incidental music.

IMPORTANT BILLING AND CREDIT REQUIREMENTS

If you have obtained performance rights to this title, please refer to your licensing agreement for important billing and credit requirements.

CADILLAC CREW was first produced by Yale Repertory Theater (James Bundy, Artistic Director; Victoria Nolan, Managing Director) in New Haven, Connecticut on April 26, 2019. The performance was directed by Jesse Rasmussen and Tori Sampson, with sets by Jessie Chen, costumes by Matthew R. Malone, lights by Kathy A. Perkins, sound by Andrew Rovner, projections by Rasean Davonte-Johnson, vocal coaching by Ron Carlos, and dramaturgy by Amy Boratko and Sophie Siegel-Warren. The production stage manager was Olivia Louise Tree Plath. The cast was as follows:

RACHEL . . . . Chalia La Tour
ABBY . . . . Dria Brown
DEE. . . . . Ashley Bryant
SARAH. . . . . Brontë England-Nelson

CHARACTERS

In Order of Appearance

RACHEL – A powerhouse of a young WOMAN. Polished. Poised. Witty. Lovingly stern. Proud.

Twenty-six years of sage. BLACK.

Actor will embody **ALICIA**.

ABBY – A powerhouse of a young WOMAN. Driven by personal goals. Values the autonomy she's never experienced. Sharp. Unapologetic.

Twenty-two years of sage. BLACK.

Actor will embody **OPAL**.

DEE – A powerhouse of a young WOMAN. Grounded in personal constitution. Mature. Hesitancy and confidence often reveal themselves simultaneously.

Sophisticated.

Thirty-five years of sage. BLACK.

Actor will embody **PATRISSE**.

SARAH – A powerhouse of a young WOMAN. Down to earth. Firm in stance and address. Protective. Secure in the past; optimistically awaits the future.

Twenty-eight years of sage. WHITE passing.

Actor will embody **JOURNALIST**.

SETTING

This play takes place in a local civil rights office. Whether that is realized or not, audiences should feel the atmosphere.

We meet these women in their native Richmond, Virginia. "Passive Resistance" has just been overturned and not everyone is happy about it. The smell of fresh cut grass, blossoming flowers and constant protests permeate the hot, sticky air.

TIME

It's mid-1963.

AUTHOR'S NOTES

Although this play is inspired by real events and people, it remains a piece of fiction.

LANGUAGE

All women are proudly southern: wearing ah "kill 'em with kindness" air as often as possible: Translation: *almost* undetectable sarcasm.

The language in the play is written to be performed in constant motion. The office scenes must be full of activity. Posters being made, typing, trips back and forth to desks, stuffing envelops, making seating charts.

With the precision of educated women, the text:
Should ricochet from one player to the next and maybe a wall or two in between. Should breathe beyond the popularized idea of women from this era.

(–) Indicates the cutting off of language
(/) Indicates the overlapping of text

VIRGINIA. 1963

Early Spring / Early Summer

(In the dark: We hear something reminiscent of "Feelin' Good" by Nina Simone.)*

(Lights up.)

(Anti-rape paraphernalia crowds the space of this local civil rights office. Signs read: "Sexual violence IS violence" "My body is not your commodity" "Sex is always consensual.")

(This office is noticeably makeshift, functional and welcoming. At Rachel's station there is a line of fruit (which she will devour by show's end). A stack of unfinished posters lay next to her desk.)

(A coffee maker and all the fixins should be accessible for all.)

*(**RACHEL** at her desk finishing typing the last agenda. She gathers the four freshly typed*

---

* A license to produce *Cadillac Crew* does not include a performance license for "Feelin' Good." The publisher and author suggest that the licensee contact ASCAP or BMI to ascertain the music publisher and contact such music publisher to license or acquire permission for performance of the song. If a license or permission is unattainable for "Feelin' Good," the licensee may not use the song in *Cadillac Crew* but should create an original composition in a similar style or use a similar song in the public domain. For further information, please see the Music and Third Party Materials Use Note on page iii.

pages and with gusto places one on each of the desks in the office. Every few seconds the word "Today" escapes her mouth.)

*(It's hot. **RACHEL** moves to lift a window open. "Hoots" and "hollers" of protesters intrude. She closes the window.)*

*(**ABBY** enters, showing off her convocation attire. She looks good.)*

*(Removes a <u>hammer</u> from her purse, stashes it in her desk, begins stuffing programs. Noticing the windows, **ABBY** opens them.)*

MOVEMENT ONE

RACHEL. T-minus six hours!

ABBY. Rachel

I know what today is

> *(The phone rings twice.* **RACHEL** *instructs* **ABBY** *to answer it.)*

Virginia Office for Civil Rights. Abby here.
Hello? Hello?

RACHEL. Programs.
Don't worry about that.

> *(***ABBY*** *hangs up.)*

ABBY. I'm stuffing. I'm stuffing.

RACHEL. Clear skies, thin clouds.
Gonna be a bright one.

> *(***RACHEL*** *grabs some cardboard, a stencil and a marker.)*
>
> *(She begins to make a poster.)*

ABBY. Mmm.
Feels like a storm's brewing outside if you ask me.

> *(Motioning to the door.)*

Been out there protesting the schools reopening all week.
They civilized now, but just you wait –

RACHEL. For what?
Found another cold bullet taped to the front door this morning.
That, along with them calls lately –

ABBY. I thought things would've died down by now.
But these fools –

RACHEL. Virginia wants to be a time capsule.
Watch the rest of the country evolve
and this state would rather be a museum.

ABBY. We're consistent if nothing else.

RACHEL. Not today! Today
Rosa Parks is coming!
Today
we move forward!

ABBY. Red, Yellow, Black and White are in these streets
asking for the same thing: Tradition.
You thank *one* woman – powerful as she might be – is
gonna roll in here and change dey minds?

RACHEL. THE woman who looked a White rapist in the
eye, telling
him he could only have his way with her corpse
as she calmly read a newspaper across the room from
him. <u>That</u> woman?

ABBY. Borderline psychotic how much you know about
someone you've never even met.

RACHEL. When you live an important life, people tend to
care about its details.

ABBY. *(Cautiously.)* Well?
Did he rape her?

RACHEL. You really wanna know?

(*A thought overtakes* **ABBY**.)

ABBY. I guess I'd rather be raped and live with the
nightmare than
a man take my body <u>and</u> soul the same day.

RACHEL. If it <u>were</u> made for you to choose...how
    <u>would</u> you die?

ABBY. Oohh, GIVING some long,
    passionate,
    highly favored
    lovin'!
    Amen?

        (The phone rings.)

RACHEL. Tame yo'self, Abby.

ABBY. I will not.

        (**RACHEL** *answers the phone.*)

RACHEL. VACR
    Rachel speaking.
    (With admiration.) Dr. Dorothy Height, how are you?

ABBY. *(Impressed.)* Again?

        (**ABBY** *moves to the coffee maker, pours a cup.*)

RACHEL. Yes, I've given thought to your car coalition...
    But, you see, Rosa Parks and I have...political plans.
    Plans on a larger scale, you see.
    Sure, keep calling and asking if you want to. *Persistence
    squanders resistance.*
    Stay safe. Bye, now.

        (**ABBY** *hands the cup of coffee to* **RACHEL.**)

        (Goes back to pour herself one.)

ABBY. My college friends from Hampton joined one dem
    Cadillac Crews.
    On dey way from Florida this week.
    Say Dr. Height organized all women, every step of the
    way,

instigating social change in the south.

RACHEL. I'm looking for something larger –

ABBY. You so picky –

RACHEL. Revolutionary.

ABBY. Two White, two Negro in every car, stopping
in the most segregated cities,
equipping willing women with integration practices.
That not revolutionary enough for you?

RACHEL. A revolution requires systemic change and a
verbose leader. See
now, Rosa could run for a government office and win.

ABBY. Ha!
On whose vote?

RACHEL. That's a minor detail.

ABBY. You say Rosa's name liken to Mother Mary or
something.
Thank you got a crush on Mrs. Parks.

(**RACHEL** *throws* **ABBY** *a look.*)

I'm jus' sayin' she real pretty-like behind dem bifocals
and bunned up hair.

(**RACHEL** *throws the look with more force.*
ABBY *catches it.*)

RACHEL. In my bones, I can feel it.
Rosa's the one gonna take us to the next level, Abby.
She's brilliant, firm, assertive –

(*Phone rings.* **RACHEL** *answers.*)

VACR.
Rachel speaking.

Yes! And I'm delighted to say that our first EVER woman speaker, Mrs. Rosa Parks, will be our keynote at today's convocation.

The subject of anti-rape activism.

Indeed, this <u>is</u>

a civil rights issue.

(*Dryly.*) Yes. Pastor Matthews will also be speaking.

Half hour maybe.

I agree, he is a bit long winded but –.

He *does* tend to spit when he preaches, however – ...

May

I suggest you sit a bit further back?

> (*Beat.*)

Not sure *all* sinners gather together by the back door.

No, Ma'am, I cannot ask him to switch to Colgate.

This is the Virginia Office for Civil Rights not a concierge service.

> (**RACHEL** *looks to* **ABBY** *to display her frustration.*)

No ma'am, not getting fresh with you.

Not getting loud either. Simply trying to expla –.

> (*Beat.*)

Hello? Hello?

She hung up.

> (**RACHEL** *drops the phone in its cradle, point to the college pennants displayed over her station.*)

Summa cum laude with a business degree from Fisk.

Masters from Howard –

ABBY. (*Rolling her eyes.*) You don't say?

RACHEL. We're here to uphold the Civil Right's Act of
     1960.
     Just last week we successfully registered six Negroes in
     this county / alone.

ABBY. Define successfully.

RACHEL. Their papers are in.

ABBY. So are yours
     and mine.

RACHEL. Point is I don't have time to be marking seating
     arrangements.

ABBY. That's why I don't answer the phones.
     We need a secretary in here to deal with all that mess.

RACHEL. That's why we hired you.

ABBY. Hired?
     You referring to that dismal check you hand me every
     month?

RACHEL. Everybody has to do their part for the / Cause.

ABBY. Cause. /
     My concern lies in what this *Cause* is doing to my
     pockets.
     I have a law degree.

RACHEL. Pre-law.

ABBY. Well ain't you overflowing with charm today.
     This is supposed to be a transition job for me.

RACHEL. Abby, this isn't a job,
     it's a <u>calling</u>.

ABBY. Sweetie, well you done dialed the wrong number.

RACHEL. Where was all this mouth when you were fresh
     outta college begging for an internship?

ABBY. When I agreed to bestow my talents here after I
   graduated
   it was predicated upon your promise of more agency
   – a chance to flex and climb. Never did you say I'd be
   pushing papers and orchestrating field trips.
   I'm sorry, Rachel, but tedious work bores me.
   I'm a visionary.

RACHEL. In due time. Is that not what I said?

ABBY. You said, <u>soon</u>.
   That's what you said.
   (Quoting RACHEL.*) The man who does more than he is
   paid for will soon be paid for more than he does.*

RACHEL. Napoleon Hill.

ABBY. <u>He</u> might've said it to someone else but *you* said it
   to *me*.
   It's you I hold accountable for my lack of *receivable*
   accounts.

RACHEL. How's it going, job training the teenagers?
   You created that program and now you're bored by it?

ABBY. I love the challenge of constructing the big ideas.
   It's the day-to-day implementation that puts me to
   sleep.

RACHEL. How can I help?

ABBY. Money.

RACHEL. Those sit-in, pickets and marches, you love to
   applaud, are mighty expensive.
   Bail money and <u>actual</u> lawyers, Abby.
   So for <u>us</u>
   this <u>is</u> community activism.
   Grass roots.

ABBY. That's what I'm down to...hot combing my own
   roots.

Look at these delicate hands.
They are forming ugly muscles!

RACHEL. What a travesty.

ABBY. You tease but I'm serious.
Put my name on the marquee at the beginning of the day or
don't fix your lips to ask me for anything else.
Ma Rainey says she was worth half the door and ten percent more.

RACHEL. That was entertainment, show business –

ABBY. Business is business.

     (RACHEL *hands* ABBY *a marker.*)

RACHEL. Here's a marker and all the paper you need.
Write Abigail as big as you like to see it and paste it outside this office door
if it makes you feel any better.

ABBY. You thank I won't?
You thank I'd find your suggestion childish,
prompting me to land on the conclusion that your proposal was simply a response to my
infantile rant.

     (*Beat.*)

BUT YOU'RE WRONG!

     (ABBY *takes the paper and writes her name obnoxiously huge. Catches a whiff of* RACHEL *and sniffs harder.*)

What's that smell?

RACHEL. It's vanilla.

ABBY. What did you do, drown yourself in it?
Smells like a botanical garden in here.

RACHEL. Don't come in here trying to dress me down this morning.
Go outside and smell that air.
It smells mighty good.
It smells like progress.
Today is the day before tomorrow

>*(**ABBY** reveals her sign to **RACHEL** before taking it outside.)*

and tomorrow has got MY name written all over it.

ABBY. Mine looks better.

RACHEL. Five hours and forty-two minutes before she arrives.

ABBY. A <u>star</u> is etched in memories eternally.
Nobody <u>ever</u> remembers the ensemble. So.
Yeah. Ponder on that.

>*(**ABBY** leaves, returns.)*

RACHEL. Air's a bit thinner today.
Wouldn't you say?

ABBY. I've never met someone so concerned with the climate.
Let alone a person who hardly steps foot outside.

RACHEL. *(Pointedly.) Wouldn't you say?*

ABBY. I'd say it's hot and sticky.
Feels like July in March.

RACHEL. Which means we made it through February.
(As if she's quoting someone great.) Remembering the need for meat stews at Christmas
makes the July Four fruit salads taste sweeter.

ABBY. You just throw words in the air,
hope they catch some logic 'fore dey drop, don't you?

Gon' make yo' little point directly and leave me be,
woman.

RACHEL. The Civil Rights Movement will enhance the
future of this country and all its people.
Tomorrow will never look like today or yesterday.
And we're doing our part to make certain of it.
It's repugnant when anyone regards it as less than.
We're designing a proud history, Abby.

ABBY. Well, I'd like to *design* my Cadillac to run.
Need gas for that
need money for gas.

RACHEL. You need what now?
Since when has your father let a desire of yours hit the
ground? Spoiled is what you are.

ABBY. Trust, his well with me can run dry.
Very hollow and dry.
And I'm not spoiled,
just...accustomed.

> (**RACHEL** *wipes her brows and darts her eyes*
> *towards the windows.*)

RACHEL. Do I ask for much? / No.

ABBY. Yes.

RACHEL. Just that today, everyone come to the office.
Ten past nine. Where is Sarah?

ABBY. In her skin I suppose.

RACHEL. I'll ask you to leave that nastiness at the door.

ABBY. Wish I could, but –
Ahhh! Oo-oo-oo-oo Ssss!

> (**ABBY** *grabs her stomach.*)

RACHEL. You okay?

ABBY. Just give me a sec.

RACHEL. Menstrual cramps creep up on you like that.
One minute you're walking through life simple enough.

ABBY. ...Oh, yeah.
Killer cramps.

RACHEL. Next, feels like an unholy grip got hold of your uterus
and's wringing it out like a soaked sponge.
Just wringing!
And wringing!

ABBY. Rach.

RACHEL. And WRINGING!

ABBY. Quit, nah.

> (**RACHEL** *points to a bottle of pills on her desk.*)

RACHEL. Three of those and a banana will do you fine.

> (**ABBY** *gathers herself before she should.*)

ABBY. No thanks,
pain's not that bad.

RACHEL. Take 'em. I need you on your feet today.
We'll all be going back and forth to the church hall setting up and orchestrating.
Did I tell you Three / Negro Newspapers are coming?

ABBY. Negro Newspapers are coming.
Yes, you might've mentioned that a time or twenty.
Don't worry, I'll be fit.

> (**ABBY** *takes the bottle and places it down.*)

RACHEL. The tougher the bleeding pains, the cuter the genes.
That's what the elders used to say.
One day all the month-to-month suffering is supposed to pay off.

ABBY. That how it works?

RACHEL. My momma used to hurt something serious.
Gorgeous as I am, my daddy messed around and caught sympathy pains.

(**RACHEL** *hands* **ABBY** *a banana.*)

ABBY. You cute. Should've taken a date to the show last night.
Everybody was there.
They played *Rebel Without A Cause.*

RACHEL. You go with Kendrick?

ABBY. Unfortunately.

RACHEL. That dry?

ABBY. We had a nice enough time.
He's a nice enough guy.
Just not...

RACHEL. James Dean, huh?

ABBY. Could the man act? I don't know.
But he looks like *Yes, Lawd* when he's doing it.

RACHEL. You and these men.

ABBY. I like whom I like.

RACHEL. Nevermind.
I shouldn't've –

ABBY. But you did so don't go biting your tongue now.
You of all people, Rachel. I don't go around judging you.

RACHEL. Be careful. That's all I meant, you know –

ABBY. I know I put a new proposal on your desk about
    equal pay reform for the city.
    See it?

RACHEL. Mmm hmm, looks valuable.
    I had some questions about section six, marked them
    in red.
    It's back on yours.

> (**ABBY** *moves to her station, finds the
> proposal.*)

ABBY. Jesus, Rachel!
    Marked it?
    The whole page is a scarlet letter.

RACHEL. A few suggestions is all.
    It's very good.

ABBY. It's exceptional.

> (**ABBY** *hands* **RACHEL** *a message from her
> desk.*)

RACHEL. What's this?

ABBY. Jones said something about a bake sale.
    Said it was for travel money.
    Gotta happen on Saturday.

RACHEL. *(With attitude.)* Who has time to bake this week?

ABBY. Same thing I said.

RACHEL. And his response was?

ABBY. Said, "Yes, Abby, darling. A bake sale."
    Ask did I want to smack the teeth out his mouth.
    Go head and ask me.

RACHEL. Who told Jones to tell you that?

ABBY. You know they don't bother us with information.
    Just instructions.

RACHEL. Jones ain't nothing but a kid. What, nineteen?
    Twenty?
    How much knowledge does he have to be handing out
    orders?

ABBY. He doesn't need knowledge, just a third leg.

>   (DEE *enters the office letting in the noise from
>   the street. It's louder than before.* DEE *carries
>   an air of seasoned womanhood.)*

DEE. Whew! I done heard enough hollerin' today.
    First my husband and now the protesters.
    Morning, ya'll!

>   (DEE *moves to her station.)*

RACHEL. Is it still morning?

DEE. Watch yo' mouth.

ABBY. Oop. *(Snickers.)*
    Morning, Dee.

DEE. Your sign, Abby, is halfway in the dirt.

ABBY. Did you pick it up?

DEE. Uh-uh. You know I don't mess with fate.

>   (ABBY *opens the door. One foot in, the other
>   out, she adjusts the paper.)*

(Looking around.) I made it here before Sarah.
    You know I have a catering company, this office and a
    home to run.

RACHEL. I don't have any violins for you, Dee.

DEE. Debra got put on the integration list last week.
    And TODAY was supposed to be her first day at the

majority White school.
But Otis felt it was the right idea to
show his complete behind down at her old school.

RACHEL. The whole thing?

DEE. When I tell you
crack and all.

RACHEL. I hope he moisturized.

DEE. Ha!
School counselor calls me saying I need to get down
there as soon as possible.
She says run if you have to.

ABBY. Debra okay?

DEE. It's her bullheaded father they're calling me to come
get.
This man done went to the majority Negro school,
grabbed a desk and pulled it into the hallway right
outside her old classroom.
Told Debra to sit right there.
Right there in the hallway.
Shaming my baby girl like that.
Anyone come tell him – this isn't allowed, she has to go
where the list says – and the list says she's assigned to
the White school now.
Anyway, Otis shouting:
"My daughter is nobody's guinea pig!
I'll be damned if you experiment with her life!"

ABBY. Why they thought all Negros were just gonna
gleefully hop to school integration still amazes me.

(**DEE** *makes a cup of coffee.*)

RACHEL. We're sitting here just now opening doors back
up for Negro children after three years of

passive resistance and no education. Washington DC done made their decision.

DEE. This here is Virginia.

RACHEL. Meaning?

(**DEE** *acknowledges the ruckus outside.*)

DEE. As much as it's proven to.

ABBY. Otis scared bout it?

DEE. Terrified if I'm being honest.
Debra was excited 'til she saw the look on Otis' face time the letter came.

RACHEL. I can just see Otis at that school...hollering

DEE. All loud

ABBY. Stomping everywhere

RACHEL. Beating on his chest

DEE. Bird chest.
Just skin and bones.

ABBY. Ole' wiry self.

DEE. Okay. He just wants her to be safe. I know it's hard for our men.
They supposed to lead and protect our families but their legs get cut down at every turn.

RACHEL. Folks treating that list like the Grim Reaper.

ABBY. Lists everywhere.
Lists to say you can or can't sit here, eat here, walk here, live
here, speak here, dream here.
Lists everywhere.
Now they done made a list say gon' learn freely and expect folks to just jump to.

Lists carry more than we see.

People scared of lists.

DEE. Any move made out of fear is a move made in reverse.

We can't let intimidation stop the progress.

People are counting on that fear to prevail.

It's a scare tactic.

ABBY. You thank the Indians thought it was *just* a scare tactic?

Let the rec / ord show.

DEE. At least they fought.

ABBY. Look around you.

What do you call what we are doing?

> (**RACHEL** *sees this as an opportunity to interject. She clears her throat loudly.*)

RACHEL. Lounging!

DEE. Fact is… I walked her down to the *assigned* school.

They out there protesting but we managed our way through the side.

I say, "Debra, you stay in your place, you stay outta trouble."

That's what my daddy used to tell me. Hell, that's what everyone's parents taught us.

Debra cocked her head back at me, say, "Mama, I belong wherever I walk."

RACHEL. Watch out nah.

That girl ain't scared of nothing.

She'll be right fine.

ABBY. A fallacy.

You ain't got to be scared to get yo' ass whooped.

Plenty of <u>unafraid</u> people done found that out.

DEE. I took the pocket knife out my bra and put it in hers.

Say, "You gon' need this you keep talking like that."

RACHEL. You gave that girl a knife on her first day?!

DEE. Rather get a call from the sheriff than the coroner.

ABBY. Should've let Otis keep her.
One less Colored girl at the school, at the protest, signing a petition, riding a bus, sitting at a counter ain't gonna stop the buggy from rolling.

DEE. Keep lying to yourself.
The power resides in numbers.
Make no mistake, it isn't the purpose that people are latching on to.
It's the movement. The masses.
We have to show up to every front line standing <u>together</u>.
That's the key to all this.

ABBY. Why you scoldin' me?
Rachel the one who don't believe in the power of protest marches.

RACHEL. Without demands or a plan to infiltrate, it's merely a performance.
I can go to the theater for all that.

ABBY. I don't blame people like Otis for being cautious.

DEE. You got to blame him.
We start to think about the welfare of our individual families above the cause, that's when we've lost the fight.

ABBY. Lives matter, too.
Mamas didn't bring babies into this world just to be taken out in the name of the *fight or cause* or whatever you liken to call it.
If I have children, I won't allow them to do this work.

DEE. Whicho selfish butt.

ABBY. You making a fighter out of your daughter, putting her on the front lines, that's selfish.

DEE. Then why are you even here?

ABBY. Not for the good tidings and great joy of it all!

RACHEL. Here she go.

ABBY. I have bigger plans for my life than being tied to struggle.

RACHEL. Like what?

(**ABBY**'s *stuck. Should she tell them?*)

ABBY. …

…

Moving to New York

or Maine.

DEE. Negros don't live in no damn Maine.

ABBY. Trailblazer like myself don't worry bout where folks been before.

I'm gonna create a cosmetic line. Run my own business.

Be something more than a Colored woman born in 1941.

RACHEL. We're <u>all</u> working for a better future.

(**DEE** *moves to her working area, sets up the typewriter, begins to sift through a stack of loose writing paper. One grabs her eye.*)

ABBY. Nah.

Don't talk to me about the future

or the children

or the next generation

or all that <u>they'll</u> reap from <u>our</u> sowing.

We talkin' bout me. My life.

And it seems like I got to do <u>this</u> to do <u>that</u>.

Got to get this country to move past <u>this</u> stage to even know if <u>that's</u> possible.

This work is a sacrifice I'm making.

An inconvenient sacrifice.

DEE. Like I said, selfish!

ABBY. What?

Don't be looking at me like / that.

RACHEL. ....Jesus was a martyr.

DEE. Hallelujah!

Greatest one to / ever live.

ABBY. Oh! Get that mess outta here!

You want to be Jesus?!

Are you calling yourself Jesus?!

I'll be a disciple. Which one of them lived?

Was it Mark?

Put that name on / me.

DEE. Look at this right here.

(Reading.) Greetings to all.

It is not by coincidence or chance happening that our time has come.

The road has been long.

Women have done our due diligence and spearheaded more campaigns than one can count.

So the time for our uprise is now!

The time for our revolution is now!

I'd like to thank –

RACHEL. Dee, pass that – Give it to me.

DEE. *The strong men who have bravely led our people through treacherous valleys and over perilous mountains designed to keep us stagnant.*

If it weren't for their courage, hard work and bravery – recognition of our plight would cease to exist.

*For they have handed us the baton on this day, and we
shall run our race!*

(**RACHEL** *attempts to grab the paper.*)

ABBY. Who's bold enough to write that?

(**DEE** *hands the paper to* **ABBY,** *points to the
bottom.*)

Ms. Rachel Helen Christopher.

RACHEL. It's not for now.
Something I've been working on for later days. After.

ABBY. After?

DEE. What exactly do you think is going to happen?

(**SARAH** *bursts through the door, her mouth
leading the way. Removing her pocket knife
and stashing it doesn't distract her words
from spilling out.*)

SARAH. You will never believe it!

RACHEL. People think they can just mosey on in here
whenever they feel.
This is a place of business not a recreation center.

SARAH. You will NOT believe it!

ABBY. Sarah, how you suppose to know that if you don't
ever tell us?

(**SARAH** *pours a cup of water from the jug on
the table.*)

SARAH. I'm telling you they're going to say
"No."
Without warning or courtesy.
I heard it myself.

DEE. Who's gonna say no about what?

SARAH. Rosa Parks.

RACHEL. She's traveling this moment. Be here on time.
I've checked the bus route twice in the last hour.

SARAH. She might be coming but she won't be addressing
the crowd.

DEE. Well why not?

SARAH. Leadership.
I dropped by your church to gather the receipts and I
overheard them discussing how they'll
inform Mrs. Rosa Parks she's *done enough.*
That they'd welcome a speech about the boycott or bus
rides but that
women's rights, anti-rape discussion was a distraction.

ABBY. Come again?

SARAH. Said they would take it from here.
Hundreds of people are scheduled to attend.

RACHEL. Must be some misunderstanding.
Not one detail hasn't been checked ten, twenty times.
I've crossed every "t," dotted every "i."

> (**RACHEL** *paces, pulls at the neck of her blouse.*
> *She whispers to herself. "Today."*)

SARAH. I assure you there is no mistake.
If Mrs. Parks attends she will not be on that platform
but somewhere in the crowd with the rest of us.

DEE. Rachel, what does this remind you of?

RACHEL. Nononononononononononono
Because we've met and planned and discussed and
ordered.
And I waited my turn.
This was supposed to be the year.
They promised. This would be the year.

*(Silence grows along with **RACHEL**'s anger.)*

DAMNIT!

> *(The women stand in shock and silence save **ABBY**, who tip-toes her way towards a heated **RACHEL**.)*

ABBY. Does this mean we'll be getting off early today?

DEE. Girl, sit yo' ass down.

> *(The shortest of beats.)*

RACHEL. Phone calls.
Everyone.
I want answers or someone who knows how to find them.

MOVEMENT TWO

*(At the office. All women are buried in their phones. We see them pick up receivers, dial, speak, hang up, repeat. At some point **RACHEL** chooses a piece of fruit from her desk and devours it.)*

DEE. I can't get through to a single soul.

RACHEL. Keep trying.

SARAH. I left a message with Fredrick's wife.
Today of all days she "has no idea where in the world he could be."

ABBY. Lyin' ass.
Tell her you know she's lying.

SARAH. I can't do that. YOU, maybe.

ABBY. Sarah. You can't be scared of a Black woman's rage.
Believe you me, the bite is never as big as / the bark.

DEE. Do *not* listen to her.

RACHEL. Anyone get through to Pastor?

DEE. No.

SARAH. The leaders meet today, right?
Two o'clock?
We ought to just crash the meeting.

RACHEL. Oh, we can't do that.

ABBY. Why not?

RACHEL. It would break protocol.
It would be disrespectful.
We simply cannot.

ABBY. See. Rachel's not mad enough.

RACHEL. Rage doesn't mean we get to ignore all semblance of regard for our leaders.

ABBY. That's exactly what it means!

DEE. We'll be polite, respectful.

SARAH. Agreed.

RACHEL. We are not going.

DEE. Fine!

(**DEE** *slams her phone. Moves to the couch and lays out.*)

Might as well sit down right here and take a good ole nap.

ABBY. Leave some room for me to rest these aching bones.

RACHEL. Dee, why are you encouraging her? <u>You</u> know much better than all this.

DEE. What I know is that civil rights supposed to mean equality for all us. But it just don't seem to be adding up that way. They can't give us what we don't ask for.

ABBY. After all these long years of fighting are behind us, where will we stand in the grand scheme of it all?

RACHEL. Your lazy butt will always and forever be SITTING. Somewhere.

SARAH. I must say, I agree with Dee and Abby. You have to at least say your piece. All the work you've done, just to get Mrs. Parks down here. It has to count for something.

RACHEL. And it will.

SARAH. When?

DEE. That's what I want to know. Rachel, they didn't even consult you.

Didn't even for one second consider what you might have to say on the matter.

Not one somebody thought to pick your brain.

ABBY. Probably pondered it real quick.

Remembered you had

lips, hips and manicured fingertips.

Thought gone.

RACHEL. Ya'll speaking to me as if I'm some persuadable child in need of direction but isn't able to receive it unless

wrapped in a personal blow to my ego.

How terribly unfortunate that you've wasted

so much energy on a pitiful attempt at / blandishment.

ABBY. Dictionary Dan over here is about to have my head hurting.

SARAH. We're saying you have merit. Especially when it comes to rallying people up.

Everyone around here sees you as a leader. Lessen, you're standing behind a man.

ABBY. When you start biting that tongue.

RACHEL. I don't bite my tongue. I'm strategic.

DEE. *Strategic.* A fancy word for *not gonna accomplish diddly-squat today.*

RACHEL. Well thank you ALL for *strategically* performing your duties in this office!

It's been a real asset.

SARAH. What do you propose we do, Rachel?

RACHEL. First off, there will be no hoopin', hollerin' and finga-swangin'.

Who here knows the full story? Huh? Exactly.

We will conduct ourselves as ladies of the movement...

not ladies of the night.

ABBY. Why must you glance my way when saying that?

DEE. In accordance, we should keep this a private matter.
No need broadcasting what we ourselves are not clear about.

RACHEL. Thank you, Dee.

ABBY. Leadership is dandy when Rosa chants about the evil White man forcing himself into the Black woman's body.
Soon as she lays facts about how the same attacks happen within our community
That's when they have issues.

DEE. How you know that's what all this is about?
You don't know that.

ABBY. Look at the context, Dee.
They got us lookin' like boo-boo's fools!

SARAH. Hard time believing this is all spur of the moment.
That we weren't being strung along for months.

RACHEL. They wouldn't do that. Not to me.

ABBY. And who are you?

(*They all glare at* **ABBY.**)

I'm just sayin' what dey thankin'.

RACHEL. Eleven years ago I joined up.
The youngest secretary.
I <u>am</u> leadership.

SARAH. Tell that to Jones.
Now they got him giving the keynote and I know that child didn't cough up a ten-page address in the last hour.

ABBY. Ohhh! Now that's triflin' on the grandest of levels.

(*To* **RACHEL**.) How many years you been asking to get on that podium?
Two?
Two and a half?

SARAH. Abby.

ABBY. Three?

SARAH. Read the room.

ABBY. Four.

DEE. Abby, stand down!

> (*A paralyzed* **RACHEL** *tries to utter. It's in vain.*)

SARAH. Rachel? Rachel?

> (**SARAH** *moves to comfort* **RACHEL**. *It's intimate and soothing until she feels the questioning energy of* **ABBY** *and* **DEE**.)

RACHEL. (*Waving* **SARAH** *off.*) Please don't touch me.

ABBY. Don't be shamed by us.
Gon' head and live your life.

SARAH. It's not what you / think.

RACHEL. Don't explain.

SARAH. I didn't –
Me, you don't mind getting mad at.

> (*The phone rings.* **RACHEL** *moves to answer it and escape* **SARAH**.)

RACHEL. (*With optimism.*) See! That's somebody calling back.
We're going to get all this smoothed out real nice.
VACR
Rachel speaking.

DEE. Who / is it?

ABBY. Who is / it?

SARAH. Who is it?

RACHEL. Hello, Jones.

DEE, SARAH & ABBY. Ah, hell!

> (**RACHEL** *listens to the chatter in the receiver for a moment.*)

RACHEL. The bake sale is not a problem.
However, I've heard that Mrs. Parks will be told not to –
Well.
What I'm saying is I sure would have liked to be included in the decision making.
Seeing that it was my word that brought her commitment to attend in the first place. Please put Pastor on the phone or Fredrick or –.
Busy?
Tell them that Rachel would –.
Don't you Darlin, me, Jones!
Calm down?
Calm down?!

ABBY. Uh-oh.

RACHEL. Jones. You know what your problem is?
You don't have any mutha –

> (**DEE** *dashes to the phone and yanks the cord from the wall.*)

SARAH. We're gonna need a new plan.

SAME PLACE. HOURS LATER

(Within the shift we should see **RACHEL** *rip signage, storm out. The others should deconstruct all the work (posters etc.) constructed in the first act. The story of defeat.)*

(No more is the robust movement and energy from the first movement.)

(No more are the posters, flyers, programs, etc., scattered about. They might reside in a corner or a trash bin. The women tidy up.)

ABBY. Since no one else is gonna say it, I will.
We should not attend the convocation tonight.
Not without Rachel.

DEE. Rachel will come back.

ABBY. Why? After Fredrick took Jones' side.
She stormed outta here like her feet were on fire.

DEE. They showed up, discussed.
Heard her out.
Just didn't see eye to eye.

SARAH. I've never seen her get that upset.

ABBY. Embarrassed is what she was.
A grown woman being put in her place by a pimply faced teenager.

DEE. She was rough.
You can't approach a man as a man.
Next time she has to come from a sugary place.

ABBY. Safe to say that cane is all tapped out.

DEE. A more generous demeanor.

Should've let her hair down, frosted her lips a little.

ABBY. Well damn.
How much are you selling her / for?

DEE. You know what I mean.
Rachel could use some softening.
Compliment a man every once in a while
even if she don't like them.

SARAH. She *offered* Jones juice and crackers.
Now that was funny.

DEE. Mrs. Parks will be invited as keynote for the NAACP women's luncheon in the fall. So it wasn't a complete loss. Rachel will still get her lady speaker and has more time to plan.

SARAH. That luncheon is a bona fide insult.

ABBY. The steam behind these open convocations is unmatched. Last one alone brought close to 800 attendees. Kings are made on that stage. Fredrick and Jones are fully aware of the implications of rejecting Rosa's voice and won't admit to their own reasoning. That's what drove Rachel out of here.

SARAH. Rachel's the one who convinced me to start volunteering.
In twenty years would I be gratified with where I planted my feet today?
Walked right up to my door and asked me that question.

DEE. Neighbors probably took her for the help.

> (**SARAH** *clocks* **DEE***'s comment. Decides to not engage.*)

SARAH. If she doesn't return, we won't know how to continue.

DEE. What do *we* look like to you?
Ran over buzzard meat?

SARAH. I just meant Rachel is our galvanizer.
   She's –

ABBY. Your favorite.
   Lightin' up whenever she gives you a project to work
   on.

SARAH. The woman has charisma.

ABBY. Agreed. Until she doesn't; exhibit A.

DEE. She'll calm down, regroup and start anew.
   She always does.

   (*SARAH moves to the door.*)

SARAH. I'm worried.
   Maybe she needs some company.

ABBY. You married, right?

SARAH. Engaged.
   Sure I told you that before.
   Twice.

DEE. She's hard of hearing words that don't come out her
   own mouth.

SARAH. Figured that much on my first day.

ABBY. Careful now, Dee...
   Your wrinkles are beginning to show.

DEE. I'm thirty-five.

ABBY. I know.
   (*To* **SARAH**.) Yo' man fine with you steppin' to the Black
   side?

SARAH. Ernest has no choice in the matter. I'm a
   liberated woman.

ABBY. What's that supposed to tell us about you?

That mean you one of those women who don't shave or wax... ANYWHERE? Girl, that's nasty.

You need to un-liberate / yourself.

SARAH. It means I don't ask anyone for permission or forgiveness.

Clair Leraux, my grandmother, helped to get women the right to vote in '20.

She marched and protested in the streets of Washington to uphold constitutional voting rights.

Opposed by many. Regard for none. That's her motto.

<u>Clair Leraux</u>.

Rachel never mentioned her name?

DEE. Why would she?

SARAH. ...

...

Grandmother is very influential is all.

DEE. Well that's cute

ABBY. For you.

DEE. Must we point out that you looking at two women that don't know what a ballot box looks like.

SARAH. Yes, of course. That's the entire reason I'm here. To help change that.

I apologize that my family pride came off as inconsiderate.

ABBY. We used to have mock elections in grade school. We'd

read all up on the presidential candidates.

Come November,

teachers hand out sheets of paper and we'd cast our vote. If

our candidate won,

swear we thought we had a hand in it.

DEE. What school was that?

ABBY. Elba Negro School on
   West Marshall
   Silly, right?

DEE. Least you had something close to the feeling.
   Been down to city hall seven times.
   Be nice to at least know what's on the paper.

ABBY. Shoot, I wouldn't vote even if this place allowed it.

SARAH. Now why would you say that?

DEE. 'Cause she adores saying simple notions so people
   will ask her to explain her simple lies.

ABBY. Who am I going to vote for?
   It makes no difference who wins.
   When it comes down to it they're all going treat us the
   same.
   Like we're invisible.

SARAH. That's what White women thought for a while,
   but it's about numbers!
   Voting means power and power means attention.
   Now, I know you like that.

ABBY. Chile, you ain't never lied!

SARAH. If the polls say women are leaning this way, the
   other party starts luring us to their side.
   It's like a huge game of courting and everyone wants to
   take you to the dance.

      (**SARAH** *turns on the radio, finds a pop music*
      station.)*

---

* A license to produce *Cadillac Crew* does not include a performance license for any third-party or copyrighted music. Licensees should create an original composition or use music in the public domain. For further information, please see the Music and Third Party Materials Use Note on page iii.

ABBY. They're just after you like that?
Finding out what makes you moan and what makes you yawn?

SARAH. Aggressively.

DEE. Well I'll be damned.

ABBY. Imagine having the United States government courting after you.

(**SARAH** *grabs* **ABBY***'s hand and they begin to dance.* **SARAH** *spins* **ABBY***.*)

SARAH. Nice, right.

DEE. Before ya'll start to tearing off clothes and whatnot.
Let us remember that Colored men can't even walk in there without trouble yet.
It'll be some time before *you* waltz in there like so.

(**DEE** *turns the radio off.*)

ABBY. We ought to call you *Stormy Dee.*
Just pouring all over our make believe parade.
Try listening to the whistles and the cheers.
Sound lovely.

DEE. Just saying
Be realistic.

ABBY. Thas depressing!
You're the one always singing about change and now you're whistling something different.

DEE. Same tune. Same melody.
You're the ones tryna skip notes.
Trust the process, *that* is what I'm saying.

SARAH. Colored men will vote. Soon, I think.
That Dr. King is gonna make sure the laws in all states – across the board – are congruent and followed.

ABBY. If he doesn't get killed first.

DEE. Now who's opening clouds?

ABBY. They got thousands of people rolling into DC. Soon.
Broadcasting everywhere that King is gon' be the main
speaker.
Now, everyone who loves him gon' be there right next
to the people who hate him.
Equal access.

SARAH. Well when you put it like that.

ABBY. I know Coretta has to wake up everyday like "Martin,
if you don't sit yo' hyper butt down somewhere!
Let Malcolm run the streets.
He got the whole Nation of Islam protecting him.
You carrying a Bible.
Last time I checked, dem ain't bullet proof."

SARAH. I don't think she would say any of those words.

ABBY. Yes she does.
Behind closed doors I bet she lets that Alabama loose
on Martin.
She's subtle enough to lead from behind but you best
believe Coretta's making decisions too.

DEE. Half the time those men are up there speaking and
I'm staring at the box like *I wonder what Betty and
Coretta have to say about all this.*

ABBY. To be a fly on the wall of those bedrooms.

SARAH. My girlfriend heard her sing in Boston.
Says she has the voice of an angel.

DEE. Hand before God, we'd be listening to her on the
radio if she wasn't a preacher's wife.

ABBY. Imagine that. (*Announcer's voice.*) The Apollo
presents: Coretta Scott!

(ABBY begins to sing something along the lines of "I Will Follow Him" by Peggy March.)*

DEE. And

theeeeeeeeeeeeeeeeeeeeeeeee

Scottettes!

(DEE and SARAH join in with "Oohs" and "Ahhs." ABBY lets them belt out a few before...)

ABBY. Naw! Coretta don't need no back-up, now!

SARAH. We sound good.

Just dreaming it up.

(SARAH and DEE keep singing.)

ABBY. Dream from your seats in the audience.

Let that woman shine!

She needs no accompaniment!!

SARAH. Who says you get to be Coretta anyway?

(SARAH moves to grab the imaginary microphone from ABBY.)

DEE. That's what I'm saying.

(DEE grabs the microphone from SARAH.)

ABBY. *You* too old and *you* too white! So time and melanin. Thas who said it!

(The phone rings again. ABBY answers it. SARAH and DEE sing.)

---

* A license to produce *Cadillac Crew* does not include a performance license for "I Will Follow Him." The publisher and author suggest that the licensee contact ASCAP or BMI to ascertain the music publisher and contact such music publisher to license or acquire permission for performance of the song. If a license or permission is unattainable for "I Will Follow Him," the licensee may not use the song in *Cadillac Crew* but should create an original composition in a similar style or use a similar song in the public domain. For further information, please see the Music and Third Party Materials Use Note on page iii.

VACR
Abby, here. Hey,
Joanna.
We still on for tomorrow –.
Calm down, I can't hear you.
You gotta stop screaming. Slower now.
Livvy what?

(**ABBY** *motions for* **DEE** *to turn on the radio.*)

(**DEE** *scans radio until she hears audible voices.*)

RADIO VOICE CRAIG. We're just getting news that's… Sammy, yeah, I dunno, so much of this is simply horrifying.

Details are coming in slowly but what we know so far is what?

(*A shaken up* **RACHEL** *enters.*)

RADIO VOICE SAMMY. Oh, yeah, we know that two White, two Negro women were, what they believe, have been shot and then burned to death on the side of a Tallahassee, Florida highway.

ABBY. (*Into the phone.*) Let me call you back.

RADIO VOICE SAMMY. Sources say the women, driving back to Maryland, identified as a Cadillac Crew:

An initiative to desegregate southern states by uniting its women.

I mean, this is an absolute tragedy. The husbands of these gals…

Do we know if they were married?

(*Somewhere between "women" and "married," the radio is turned off by* **RACHEL**.)

(**DEE** *moves to comfort* **ABBY**, *she refuses.*)

RACHEL. News already spreading like fire.

No names.

Today, they sayin' four women.

Tomorrow, they forget the number and just say *a handful.*

Ten years, fifty years from now it'll say people.

Just *people*.

No photos, press, news articles following the journey.

They're burned to a crisp…fighting for this country… with no record.

No Names!

ABBY. *(Under her breath.)* Henrietta and Livvy. Henrietta and.

Olivia Nobles.

Got thick eyebrows and, uh, small feet.

Size, size, four… I believe.

No one in the dorm could ever trade shoes with her, her feet so small.

Good dancer too. Real good. Could pick her laugh from a crowd it was so unapologetic.

Henrietta Shire is…was, uh, uh, she liked to

talk about birds…a lot. Wanted to travel the world just to see new ones.

Birds. Philadelphia. She's from Philadelphia.

Has a brother who's deaf so she knows…knew

sign language.

See.

She taught me to say my name.

(**ABBY** *spells her name in the air.*)

Two names right there.

So you can quit referring to them as <u>burned to a crisp</u> and call them Henrietta and Livvy.

(*The wheels begin to turn for* **RACHEL.**)

RACHEL. How about pioneers? Women of the movement? Crusaders?
It isn't enough for a handful of people to know a handful of facts.

DEE. Show some respect.

RACHEL. What? They knew the ride was risky.
Issue isn't that they're dead…it's that sixty years from now the world won't know how.

DEE. These are people, human beings.
Abby's actual, factual friends.

RACHEL. Right.
Friends with no legacy.

(*Wheels turn faster.*)

ABBY. Rachel! Don't you dare!

RACHEL. But <u>we</u> can change that. For them.

(**RACHEL** *lands on something.*)

<u>We</u> can make this right.
Do this drive the correct way.
The four of us.

SARAH. Excuse me?

RACHEL. (*With gusto.*) We'll transcribe everything.
Write to the papers.
All keep separate journals.
Demand that we be seen and heard.
Abby, you a visionary right?

(*Silence.*)

(**RACHEL,** *anxious and ignited, moves to* **ABBY**.*)

How do you want to die?
I'm serious.
We're all going one way or another.
Only promise you can count on.
C'mon. C'mon.

DEE. Stop this! Can't you see the girl is in shock?

>   (*Ignoring* **DEE**, **RACHEL** *intensely zones in on* **ABBY**.*)

RACHEL. Huh?
Want your name to mean something one day right?
Well this is how we do it. This is how we get our names and work out there.
Because if we stay here...
(*To* **DEE**.) Under all these men we gon' end up no better than Claudette.

DEE. Shit, Rachel.
ENOUGH!

RACHEL. Her name matters, Dee!

DEE. Since when?

RACHEL. Fine.
Want me to hold history from you, Abby, I'll be silent.
Keep it under the rug for people to walk all over.
Just pretend it didn't happen until we all forget.

>   (*Beat.*)

ABBY. You know I want to know.

>   (**DEE** *silently / angrily resigns.*)

RACHEL. Nine months before Rosa, Claudette,
a Montgomery girl, refused to give up her seat on a city bus,
Leading to her arrest. Courageous teenage girl.

No status, no ties or connections to big leaders.
A seemingly powerless woman they thought.
Turns out
she was vital in the case argued at the Supreme Court.
Claudette was a brave pioneer and a heck of a spokesperson.

SARAH. But Mrs. Parks –

DEE. Was established.
Also not an unmarried, <u>pregnant</u> teenager.
Folks felt it was best not to publicize Claudette's involvement in the movement.
Thought her condition would be an embarrassing distraction.

(The phone rings.)

(ABBY answers.)

ABBY. Hello?
I'll have her call you back.
What folks?

RACHEL. Not that we had any power back then, I was just starting out myself.
But when talks occurred I can admit I supported the decision they made to shield her from
the / public eye.

ABBY. You mean they pushed her out for being pregnant?

DEE. More complicated than that.
At the time, it's what everyone thought was best for the collective image.
The Alabama leaders made a choice and the rest of the chapters followed suit.

RACHEL. How could we afford to gamble that much from so far behind.

It was parlous.

SARAH. Can't see how very much has changed.

ABBY. In them or ya'll.

RACHEL. I was wrong.
I see that now.
Jones, Fredrick, Pastor...all of them are acting as if we haven't been there from the beginning.
Before we even had a table...sitting on stoops, pews, restaurant booths...
I always had a seat. But –

DEE. Now they done pushed you out and you want to risk OUR lives to make a point.

RACHEL. An invisible line has been drawn that we're not permitted to cross.
Doors we don't have keys to.

DEE. – Big as your chest is right now –
This isn't about anyone but you and those grand speeches you've been typing up.

RACHEL. We can do this!
This is about the group.
All of us are going to grab hold of this civil rights movement.
We are going to literally *drive* our women's agenda right next to the Negro one.
State by State!

SARAH. We could champion voting rights for Colored women!

RACHEL. Exactly.
This cycle where we allow ourselves to be placed in the peripheral of our own fight has come to an end! We can lead an improved revolution where women have the opportunities to stand front and center.

DEE. There is nothing wrong with <u>where</u> we stand.
Sure, let's stand higher, speak louder.
A revised mutual agenda should be implemented,
however, men *are* more suited to lead.

RACHEL. I'd beg to differ and challenge to prove otherwise.
No more
will we only be called upon for the female perspective.
I have thoughts from my human perspective.
From my American perspective.

DEE. That's the goal,
to make sure they're one in the same.
That's what we should be pushing for.
Not two battles but
one
all encompassing.

ABBY. Now that there sounds like the way to go.

DEE. Thank you.

RACHEL. The truth is nobody is going to make space for us
to merge. Not in this lifetime.
We either stand up or accept invisibility.

ABBY. Hmm. Good point.

DEE. How you know that? We just started asking for more
a hot minute ago. Give it time.

RACHEL. How much? Give me an answer and I'll consider
your view. How much time do you think it'll take to be
seen? Heard? Respected? Valued? Huh? How much
time Dee?

ABBY. Good question.

DEE. *(Et tu Brute?)* Abby?

ABBY. When we gon' get to taste the America we were
promised?

What Rachel preaching sounding mighty nice.

Negro women speaking not just for ourselves but on behalf of our nation, *in front of our nation.*

RACHEL. Acknowledging our womanhood in our stance.

DEE. Our gender is apparent. It doesn't need to be spoken of.

That's where you move into dangerous territory.

Only so many ways this country can be split and still *BE* a country.

RACHEL. As it stands now

the split exists vertically.

I'm suggesting that we refocus it horizontally

allowing people to advocate for themselves.

DEE. ...

...mmm-hmmm.

riiiight.

RACHEL. You're resisting the empowerment of your identity and –

DEE. My identity?

I'm Black

and happen to be a woman.

ABBY. No.

You're a woman who happens to be Black.

Right, Sarah?

SARAH. Don't do that, Abby.

I'm hardly qualified to speak on the matter.

ABBY. We also can't afford for you to slip out of this discussion.

You wanted to do the work, well this is it.

Name a successful social or economic shift in this country that wasn't supported by a faction of White brothers and sisters.

You're not just qualified.
You're essential.

SARAH. You're saying my Whiteness is essential.
Not me in particular.

DEE. *(Snappily.)* No truer words have left those lips.

RACHEL. What you represent, Sarah, is power.
Power that we – circumstantially, momentarily – lack.
If you can admit to that, I can admit to your importance
in *our* pursuit of it.

> (**SARAH** *begins to view her social mapping
> from a different angle. She likes it.*)

SARAH. I feel like I should say you're welcome?

DEE. What an honor it must be for you.
So welcome to OUR

RACHEL. Dee.

DEE. Dee the Negro or Dee the woman?

RACHEL. Dee the parent of a twelve-year-old girl.

DEE. So mother.

ABBY. She said parent.

DEE. Would you ask Otis to consider the same thing?

RACHEL. I'd beg Otis to consider it.

DEE. He wouldn't
and I respect him for it.
This office is geared to demolishing segregation of color
and class and here you go proposing the same system.
As long as it puts you on top.
Not worried one bit about the people you'll stomp on
to get there.

RACHEL. That's the mentality that's going to keep us
always walking one step behind Colored men,

two steps behind White women and a mile and a half behind White men.

That right there.

The mere thought that anytime we want to rise to the top, somehow that means we're pushing everyone else down a notch.

SARAH. *(To* DEE.*)* You've been fashioning strategies for interfaith and community connections for years. Yet you're classified as a volunteer.

DEE. You see I'd buy that if not just hours ago Rachel had all the respect in the world for our fearless leaders. Go ahead and admit it! Admit it!

RACHEL. This is about redesigning our political formation.

ABBY. Tempering masculinist terms of leadership –

DEE. Oh, shut that shit up!

ABBY. Dee. Be civilized.

You're fussing like a teething / child.

DEE. I'm speaking as a woman who values coalition.

ABBY. And just where has that gotten us?

DEE. Here! From way back there to right here.

Roofs over our heads, jobs, schools, churches, banks, businesses, colleges, sororities, fraternities, upward mobility, Negro middle class, two-parent households, family.

Just 'cause Rachel don't have no interest in starting one /

RACHEL. Oh, wait a second / now

DEE. Behind every great man, Rachel! BEHIND! / You're one of them baby hating women, aren't you?

RACHEL. I don't care nothing about a man / don't you dare say that to me.

(The phone rings.)

ABBY. Whoa! Whoa! Whoa!

SARAH. Too far! You've crossed the line now!

RACHEL. I love babies! And you know it.

> *(Everyone is silently dramatic. A line has been crossed.)*

> *(**DEE** answers.)*

DEE. Hello? Hello?

> *(She hangs up.)*

Got threatening phone calls, bullets taped to doors.
Every other day is another battle to overcome.
Abby, your friends died tryna do something good. I can see that.
I can see how they thought it was possible. But look what happened, huh?
The radio say they were shot and burned.
You shoot somebody
why you need to light fire to the body?
What they tryna hide?
What they do to them women they felt the need to burn away?
Ain't nobody in this room ready to walk that line.

RACHEL. Speak for yourself.

DEE. Dorothy Height. Daisy Bates. Ruby Dee.
Lorraine Hansberry. Mahalia Jackson. Ella Baker.
Septima Clark. Gloria Richardson.
Those women are surely next in line if there were to be any sort of Negro woman leadership.
Not you.

RACHEL. Says who?

DEE. Giiiiirl!

> (**DEE** *quickly walks away from* **RACHEL.** *On her heels, returns.*)

Are you sick with a brain tumor? It would explain a heck of a lot right now.

RACHEL. Nothing is growing inside my head beside God given audacity.

DEE. You prideful, arrogant, commanding, self-assured –

RACHEL. Don't stop there. My resume is much longer.

DEE. What are you going to say next?
The Lord called upon you to lead?

RACHEL. No. I called upon myself.

DEE. There it is!

RACHEL. So what!
I'm qualified!
Every molecule in my body says I'm fit to guide.
My credentials are valid, my commitment to this cause is unwavering.
I've sacrificed dignity and family.
I've bled from my head and my feet.
I've sat at counters and in jail cells.

DEE. Many of us have.
It doesn't grant any status!

SARAH. Why not? You said yourself that women deserve a larger platform.
An audible voice for the nation to hear.

ABBY. Isn't this the change you're always talking about?

DEE. Family business.
We air out our grievances at home. Doors locked.

You're talking about inviting the whole world inside
to smell our dirty laundry when they have no problem
making it themselves.

Think about the repercussions of unbearable weight
this will put on our community.

Women are supposed to be the backbone of the
movement, not the foot on the neck of it.

Now that

is an *embarrassing distraction.*

RACHEL. I won't sit back and idly watch myself be written
out of history.

DEE. And I won't commit to dying behind any woman
who doesn't have sense enough to know that our names
are hardly respected when written alone.

RACHEL. We are going.

DEE. You don't get to speak for everyone.
Sarah?

    *(**SARAH** nods.)*

SARAH. Nothing will change if we don't.
It's time, Dee.

DEE. Figures.
Abby?

ABBY. Course I don't want to end up like Henrietta and
Livvy. But I'm tired of living like this too; so low to the
ground. Dee, I gotta try something different.

    *(**DEE** grabs her purse and a stack of stuffed
    programs.)*

DEE. I'll drop these at the church.

ABBY. Dee, c'mon. We need you.

DEE. Nah.

Do what you want.

But me?

I'm going home to make my husband and child a hot dinner.

RACHEL. Have a lovely day.

DEE. DON'T TELL ME WHAT TO DO!

(**DEE** *exits.*)

(**RACHEL** *moves to the phone.* **ABBY** *and* **SARAH** *walk towards their desks.*)

(**ABBY** *reaches for her stomach, then mouth.*)

ABBY. I need to sit...ugh...

pass me a...

(**ABBY** *points to a trash bin.*)

RACHEL. Should've taken those pills.

None of that laziness.

(**ABBY** *rushes to the nearest bin but doesn't make it. She vomits. And vomits.*)

Oh, God, Abby are you sick?!

Now, why would you get sick when we've got a trip to chart out?

SARAH. Well I'm sure she didn't plan it, Rachel.

ABBY. I'm fine.

Probably just ate something funny.

RACHEL. Well shake it off then.

SARAH. She needs to sit. Relax.

RACHEL. Sure.

Relax.

Take all the time you need *in the next ten minutes.*

(**RACHEL** *reaches into her drawer, rummages, pulls out a bottle of castor oil.*)

Swallow some castor oil. It'll clean you right out.

SARAH. No ma'am.

That's the last thing a woman in –

ABBY. RACH!

I sure would love an ice-cold ginger ale right about now.

Maybe a few nickel candies?

Settle me just right. I promise.

RACHEL. *(Reluctantly.)* Back in a minute.

That's *nine* before our impromptu medical break is up.

(**RACHEL** *exits.* **SARAH** *cleans up.* **ABBY** *sits silence.*)

SARAH. Last week you turned down your favorite chicken sandwich.

Between that, your attention to smell and this

ABBY. …

SARAH. Now you know you can't join on a Cadillac Crew.

Got to tell Rachel.

ABBY. Still trying to wrap my head around.

This.

SARAH. Have you seen an obstetrician?

ABBY. I'm only a few weeks.

Not ready to walk through that door.

SARAH. Sweetie, like it or not this is happening.

ABBY. My father refuses to speak me.

SARAH. An unwed debutante.

ABBY. I know.

SARAH. Can't be surprised by that.
In the meantime, you and
Kendrick will figure it out.

ABBY. Oh, highly doubt that.

SARAH. He was parentally approved.

ABBY. Making Ethan less than ideal.

SARAH. Ethan?
I see.

ABBY. You don't.

SARAH. Give it a rest. We have our differences but I assure you
love and passion are universal desires.

ABBY. I know that.

SARAH. Do you?

ABBY. I wasn't trying to be confrontational. It's complicated because –. Huh.
Okay.
You, your fiancé and Ethan are all…
Beatles.
Me?
I'm a Supreme.

SARAH. A what?

ABBY. You know.
A *Beatle* and a *Supreme.*

> (**ABBY** *does something to exaggerate her point. It takes* **SARAH** *a beat to catch on but when she does…)*

SARAH. He's a Beatle! Ethan's White!

ABBY. Must you shout?

SARAH. I think I'm allowed to be shocked.
It's not like he came to your front door asking for your
hand.

ABBY. It's more romantic than that.

SARAH. Do tell!

ABBY. Uhh, nah. I really shouldn't. Said too much as it is.

SARAH. G'on, you know you want to.

>   (**ABBY** *never gets to tell this story. She wants
>   to.)*

ABBY. Y'know the general store down by the lazy river?

SARAH. Yeah, course.

ABBY. My girlfriends and I would go to the back door,
point
to the items we wanted.
Always three pieces of butterscotch and a peppermint
stick but
Ethan would see me eyeing these large malt balls.
One day he put one in my bag.
I thought it was a mishap so I gave it back.
Next week I found two in there. Then three. Four. Five.

SARAH. Hmm. I already like him.

ABBY. He'd add one every week until I said, "You rottin'
my teeth, man. You tryna make me ugly?"
He turned bright red, had the saddest look on his face.
And the urge to kiss him just washed over me.
So I did.

SARAH. Well aren't you a bold one.

ABBY. It's true. Something catches my good ear and can't
nobody tell me
the danger of hearing it again.

SARAH. I can't believe you're going to be a mother.

ABBY. Perhaps
    Mama knows a lady in Arlington.
    I have to get there within the next week or so…

SARAH. Abby, listen to yo'self.

ABBY. I make my own decisions, Sarah.
    I too am a liberated woman.

SARAH. There are other ways of dealing with this sorta thing. This kind of pregnancy doesn't have to be so tragic.

>   (**ABBY** *tries to hold her emotions. It's a losing battle.*)

ABBY. Ain't nothing tragic about what I got growing in me. I've felt more than hatred, pity or ambivalence from your skin.
    Not many Coloreds can say that.
    That ain't tragic, that's a miracle.

SARAH. I'm a miracle?

ABBY. You say one nice thing about White people and ya'll want a damn gold-plated cookie prize.

SARAH. I was joking!

ABBY. Sure you were.

>   (**ABBY** *puts herself back together.*)

SARAH. Rachel should be back soon.

ABBY. You and Rachel. There's a deal there.

SARAH. A deal?

ABBY. A very delicate one I presume. One that Mr. Ernest might not approve of?

SARAH. You remembered his name. I guess I'm starting to grow on you, huh?

ABBY. I've always liked you.

SARAH. ...

ABBY. You just came out of nowhere. That's all.

SARAH. I'm sure we've run into each other a time or two.

ABBY. Where?

SARAH. Somewhere. I'm sure. Natick Road, perhaps.

ABBY. What do you know about Natick Road? I live two streets over – by the pool.

SARAH. I have family there.

ABBY. Family? On Natick?

SARAH. Yes.

ABBY. Rachel stay close to Natick too.
You know that?
Yeah, you know that.

SARAH. It's complicated.

ABBY. Ain't you been listening?
Complicated lovers are my specialty.

SARAH. We. Are not lovers.

Why do you even care?

ABBY. We're getting familiar.

SARAH. You've known Rachel how long?

ABBY. Since Sister Thelma's Sunday school classes.
And I know she was more concerned with Sister Thelma than the lesson.

SARAH. We should draft an announcement.
More people who know we're coming
more people who might want to help get us there safely.

ABBY. I told you my secret.

SARAH. I figured it out.

ABBY. *(Whispering.)* With a White man's baby.

SARAH. …

ABBY. A. White. Man.
C'mon now that has to buy me something.
So you love her?

SARAH. In a way. Yes.

ABBY. And she?

> *(Silence.)*

> *(A beat.)*

> **(RACHEL** *enters without snacks. She slams
the door behind her, closes the curtains.)*

RACHEL. Dee come back?!

ABBY. Why are you empty-handed?
What's wrong?

RACHEL. Don't you hear all that?! Barely made it halfway
down the block!
They're saying it's Debra. Drew that knife on a boy at
school.
Those peaceful marches done turned into riots.

> *(The hollers and shouts get louder. We hear
bodies moving quickly in the streets.)*

ABBY. What in the world is today?

> **(RACHEL** *dials.)*

RACHEL. Dr. Height? It's Rachel. I've got a car and a crew.
Three women.

(**RACHEL** *looks to* **SARAH** *and* **ABBY** *for final approval. They nod.*)

I don't have a fourth.
Yes, we've heard the news.
And we still –.
We're determined to go if you'll still have us.
Great.
Listen, we're gonna do things a little differently.
I have some ideas…

(*Blackout.*)

MOVEMENT THREE

On the Road, in Motels, at Gas Stations, Rachel, Abby, and Sarah Write

RACHEL. To whom it may concern,

We left Virginia today.

Our Crew consists of Abigail Carmichael, Sarah Pearson and Rachel Helen Christopher. In the event that our likenesses are destroyed or distorted

I've attached marked photos of each of us.

ABBY. *Journal entry #1*

Note to self. Never leave for a road trip without comfortable pants. And ear plugs.

There's no escape on the open road and

swear 'fore God if Rachel recites another version of a "just in case" speech, I will

personally toss her typewriter from my car.

RACHEL. *Journal entry #5*

My body still tingles after delivering my very first public address! I'll admit, there is much room for improvement, especially in the way of voice power. At the moment, I lack a certain grandiose pitch but will continue to improve.

All in all, Today was a good day!

To whom it may concern,

The women in East Kentucky were mighty impressive! They'd already gathered a small coalition eager to dive right in. Over a year ago, two young ladies, Odessa Perkins and Inez Atler began hosting integrated park-time with their daughters once a month. Six mothers have since joined. I'd stand in disbelief had I not seen it with my own eyes.

SARAH. *Journal entry #11*

Two weeks we've been on the road.

Dr. Height keeps checkin' on me – concerned how I'm fairing out here without another White woman to share the load with. I've told her things I thought I'd never admit.

Like how having to sleep away from my crew,

in a Whites only hotel is the only time of day

my heart beats at a steady rate.

I tell Dorothy how

Driving on the road is terrifying.

Stopping the car – even more frightening.

How I feel every second could be my last.

How sometimes I need to take a small break – doesn't have to be long, just a respite from constantly having to be alert and prepared for anything.

I babble, she listens.

This helps.

RACHEL. To whom it may concern,

I'm pleased to inform you that we're making spectacular strides!

It is ever so clear that we, along with our efforts, are surely essential.

That being said,

I have a genius idea that I'm passing on as a suggestion:

When you write about us, please provide this address for subscribers to send donations along:

National Council of Negro Women

633 Pennsylvania Ave, NW Washington DC

Our spirits are full but our gas tank is not.

Any help folks felt moved to provide would be put to great use.

ABBY. *Journal #18*

Guess who hopped on a bus surprising us in Tennessee…

Dee!

I don't know what changed her mind, and she's hellbent on guarding those details, but I'm glad she's with us. Feels a bit safer with her around.

RACHEL. To whom it may concern,

We're still alive after our troubles in Georgia.

In Fairburn, we were met by Louise, a Negro teacher who'd been in contact with Dr. Height for some months.

Louise introduced us to Helen, a White mother and preacher's wife, who like the women in previous cities, wanted to leverage her Whiteness in pursuit of integration.

The plan remained the same as the cities prior:

Abby, Dee and I teach integration strategies and tactics to Colored women while Sarah does the same with White.

We stay only three days, two nights.

Long enough to assess the racial climate of the community, offer insight, collect data and merge the two groups into one.

On our last evening, we were ambushed by both sides.

Seems Louise and Helen were skeptics of Dr. Height's agenda and my radical speeches failed to make believers of them.

About ten women, all spewing verbal threats of bodily harm, ran us out of town real good.

The irony of segregated folks

unifying to uphold segregation baffles me.

I guess folks would rather bleed from a familiar wound than run

the risk of cutting a new one.

ABBY. *Journal #22*

Take the good where it comes. And yesterday was good. Fourteen women agreed to open their Whites only pool to Negro kids and their mothers for the last two operation hours of a day. For one month. If all goes well perhaps they'll consider a longer term arrangement.

Maybe even sharing the pool all day? After the time we had in Georgia, I'll take this as a hard fought win.

Also, today is my birthday!

Dee found the time to bake the most delicious three-layer chocolate fudge cake my taste buds have ever touched.

RACHEL. *Journal #37*

It's June 17th.

Dorothy called our host house today.

Apparently there's been another incident on the road.

This time in Texas. A crew's car was stolen but they were unharmed. Dorothy says to be ultra vigilant.

To protect our bodies before anything else.

She also asked that I pass along the news to my crew. I haven't and I won't. We all know the odds.

No need to needle it deeper.

DEE. *Journal #19*

The car smelled like a dumpster after,

within seconds of each other,

Sarah burped and

Abby pooted.

Rachel was ready to pull over

Until I started laughing uncontrollably. So much so

that the others caught it too!

There we were, in the middle of all that stink, bellowing and cackling until our faces ached and stomachs filled with cramps.

I pray our moment of joy stretched miles of road, reaching my baby girl Debra today.

RACHEL. To whom it may concern,

I delivered my tenth speech today and it felt its best. I've attached a copy.

Might you want to publish it?

Dear Washington Post,

Dear Boston Globe,

Dear New York Times,

Dear Chicago Tribune,

Dear Denver Post,

Dear Houston Chronicle,

Dear Philadelphia Inquirer,

Dear Hartford Courant,

Dear New Hampshire Gazette,

Dear Phoenix Standard,

Alaska Spotlight,

Southern Mediator Journal,

Mississippi Free Press,

Patriot,

Gazette,

Crusader,

Observer,

Journal,

Eagle,

Post,

Sentinel,

Bulletin,

Enquirer,

Have you received any of my correspondence? It's disappointing to know that you've not decided to run our story as of yet. I'm still hoping for that to change. However, if not, could you honor this one ask? Please archive my letters and photos. In a basement box will be fine. Just please don't destroy them. We know we are making history.

Journal #50

You'd think, after two months on the road, the jitters would've worn off. We just passed the *Welcome to Mississippi* sign. I don't pray very often but right now, I'm sending up a mighty one.

SHIFT. MOVEMENT FOUR

(Night. A cloud of steam escapes from the hood of the Cadillac. A set of headlights disappear in the distance. **DEE, ABBY, SARAH,** *and* **RACHEL** *are visibly shaken up.* **DEE** *stands with a gun by her side.)*

RACHEL. You pulled out a gun!

DEE. I'm not dying today! And that man, way he was looking at us...

ABBY. He was offering a ride and since we got a broke down Cadillac, you should've let us take it!

DEE. He was offering Sarah a ride! Not you!
You, he was offering a six foot hole in the ground.
He was gonna take you.

ABBY. I know.

DEE. God, you know?

ABBY. You got a better idea? Here we are in the middle of somebody's backwoods –

DEE. God, I almost lost my life after your fast-tailed behind.
Why you wanna die so bad? Tell me that, huh?
What makes life so unbearable you willing to throw it away every chance you get?

ABBY. You hollering at me when you really livid with this one!

*(***ABBY*** point to ***SARAH***. But ***DEE*** doesn't break her attention to ***ABBY***.)*

RACHEL. We don't have time to get into all that.

SARAH. Obviously you know
I meant none of those words but –

DEE. Oh, when you said we were niggers needing edifying

SARAH. No! No, I would never use that word. I said *them*.
    You know I said them, Dee!
    I couldn't not use my voice
    So I said what I had <u>to</u>.
    What I knew would keep us alive.

(**DEE** *grips her gun tighter.*)

DEE. Like I said, we aren't dying today.

SARAH. If you would just try to understand my perspective.
    I risked my life too you know –

DEE. You risked what?!
    Rachel get cho' people.

RACHEL. Stop. Okay, Sarah. Just stop it.
    We can't do this right now.
    We have to keep moving.
    Map said we're just thirty miles from Jackson.
    We'll walk if we have to.

ABBY. And leave our journals?!
    Letters?!
    That fancy voice recorder you bought?

RACHEL. Eight arms between us.
    Might as well put them to use.
    Everyone grab something.

ABBY. I ain't going nowhere away from this car.

(**ABBY** *pulls a handful of tools from the steel
    box, moves towards the car.*)

DEE. The alternator needs replacing and –

ABBY. Just let me figure it out!

DEE. You more liable to break something than fix it, Abby.

ABBY. I'm not moving away from this car. You hear me.

RACHEL. We have to!

DEE. No, we don't.
    We going from three Colored women
    and Sarah
    driving IN
    and thankfully OUT of danger
    to attempting the same thing?
    On foot?
    Nah.
    We'll lock ourselves inside this thing before we do that.

RACHEL. We stay put and we will miss our appointment at
    the Women's Club in Clinton.

ABBY. Rachel would lead us to the devil's embrace if it
    meant he'd hear her last words.
    But listen to mine: Abby ain't moving.

RACHEL. Let me fix this.
    I'll go find a payphone, get us help.

SARAH. No! You can't go off by yourself.
    We need to stick together.

ABBY. Then everybody better get mighty comfortable.
    Right here.

SHIFT

    (**RACHEL** *walking down the road.* **SARAH** *chases behind* **RACHEL**.*)*

SARAH. Hold on, will you.

RACHEL. Dee doesn't owe you anything for your heroic acts back there. None of us do.
So if gratitude is what you're looking for –

SARAH. I'm not.
Who are you going to call?

RACHEL. Dorothy.

SARAH. Grandmother's network is larger.
Women's Bureau. AAUW.
BPW. The Commission.
One call.

RACHEL. Sarah.
You don't get to decide everything just 'cause you think you should.
What was our deal?

SARAH. Look where we are!
I couldn't care less about our deal.

RACHEL. Don't you dare. I knew this would happen.
I knew, I knew, Sarah. And what did you say?

SARAH. It's not just you who has to live like this.

RACHEL. You have the audacity to hold anger. At me?

SARAH. Oh I'm sorry.
Am I bothering you with my emotions?
How dare I.
Please.
Ignore me, per usual.

RACHEL. Walk. Faster!

SHIFT

> (**DEE** *throws her head over her neck in reaction to any sound / movement.*)

ABBY. Why can't we sit in the car?

DEE. Told you. Got to be alert. We might need to run. And fast.

ABBY. They want to find us, they will. I just hope you got plenty of bullets in that thing.

DEE. Leave me alone, girl.

ABBY. You still mad at me?

DEE. I said. Leave me alone.

ABBY. Fine.

> (*Silence.*)

> (*Silence.*)

> (*Silence.*)

> (**ABBY** *whistles.*)

> (**DEE** *wants to slap her.*)

DEE. I told Otis I'd be right back.
Just going down to county jail for a visit.

> (*Silence.*)

> (*Silence.*)

ABBY. Why you go and lie to him like that?

DEE. 'Cause yo' stupidity done rubbed off on me that's why.

ABBY. Soon as we get out of here...if we –.
I'm moving up North.

DEE. Mmm. I'd like to say they'd be lucky to have you but
that's a lie.

ABBY. 'Cause I'm getting married
And it ain't to Kendrick neither.

>   (*Silence.* **ABBY** *regrets telling her truth.*)

Don't you want to know who?

DEE. I barely want to know <u>you</u>.
So, no.

ABBY. 'Cause I just ain't got no kind of good in me, right?

DEE. Not a lick.

ABBY. Debra's more like me than you.
That's how I know she'll survive in there.
However long they intend on keeping her locked up.
She'll survive.

DEE. She's nothing like you.

ABBY. You want her to be yo' mirror?
In the face of death worried about what her man gon'
thank if she
ain't home to wash his butt?

DEE. That's supposed to hurt my precious feelings?

ABBY. Yes.

DEE. Wanted my daughter to walk through the front door,
not the back.
Legally know that she belongs.
It was just a piece of paper, a list, a dream.
So when that petition rolled around,
I signed it
And jumped through all the hoops.
I put my daughter in that school, in that jail, in the face
of death.

That was all me.

And I don't even know if I harbor any regret.

All I know is

Debra thinks <u>she</u> did the right thing.

Says she did what I would've done.

How I speak about fearless living.

How I stand for something.

How because of me she couldn't let that boy harass those girls.

ABBY. You got in the car to put proof behind Debra's ideas of you?

DEE. *(With sincerity and vulnerability.)* Rachel talking about making sure we get printed up in the papers all over.

Front page.

I'd show Debra – if we ended up on a big one, the Times, Post, Globe, something credible –

That's your Mama, working for equality. Fighting for you.

If I don't do this, everything she believes about me, all the values I passed on to her, she'll see as a lie.

A lie she based the biggest decision of her young life on.

So you see, I didn't really have a choice but to get in that car when the only other options are sitting and waiting for someone else to change Debra's fate.

Getting in that Cadillac, coming on this trip is me trying to enlarge the little bit of hope she got stored up. In that moment, me seeing my daughter being carted away and wasn't nothing I could do to stop it, that's what I decided being a mother was.

She might die in there. I might die out here.

Least we can both say our lives were about trying to fulfill a purpose.

ABBY. <u>Life</u> is worth living if you know what you want to do with it.

That's the only way. Got to know what you want.
Make yourself big enough to the point where
your purpose sees you as clearly as you see it.
That's the key.

I ain't gonna <u>be</u> a business woman.
It don't see me the way I see it.
My face too blurry.
My skin too dark.
My voice too high.

DEE. You don't know that.

ABBY. I know we gon' die fighting.

(*Silence.*)

See you ain't even gon' try to set me straight on that.

(*Silence.*)

And you right, sometimes I just want to speed up the
process, speed up the pain, speed up the agony of being
blurry.
Being out of focus to the rest of the world.

DEE. You the most nerve-stomping little stick I've ever
met.
But you ain't no kind of blurry to me.
I see you.
And you <u>always</u> yapping.
Hard not to hear you.

ABBY. Just wish I could sense our future. Could feel the
air change.
'Cause then I'd know
it'll all be worth it.

(*Silence.*)

(Silence.)

(Silence.)

*(**DEE** turns her face so **ABBY** can't see the tears falling from her eyes.)*

Thank you for saving me.

DEE. Shut up lil girl.

ABBY. And my baby.

DEE. What you say?

SHIFT

SARAH. Be smart, Rachel. Swallow your pride and call
   grandmother.
   You <u>know</u> she'll get us off this road quicker than anyone
   else could.
   It's more than you!
   Dee has a family!
   Abby is pregnant!

SHIFT

DEE. So dramatic. "And my baby."
I hope it's a girl so you get back all the nonsense you done put out.

ABBY. What about Celia?

DEE. That's an old name, sturdy but old.

ABBY. Clara?

DEE. Plain.

ABBY. Your name is the fourth letter in the alphabet and got the nerve to call *Clara* plain.

DEE. It's short for Debra.

ABBY. You named your daughter after you?

DEE. I carried her, labored her, let her crack my pelvis wide open and stretch my skin from east to west –

(**ABBY** *cringes and talks to her belly.*)

ABBY. You won't do that to your pretty mama now will you?

DEE. Yes! Say, yes I will.
After all that, Debra Jr., is what I wrote on that birth certificate.

ABBY. Right now I want to see my baby's face more than anything.
Haven't always felt that way.

DEE. You'll be her hero.

ABBY. I want more than that!
I want more than motherhood to put my pride in.
I know you think I'm selfish but I don't want to die in the number.

I need to believe that I'm possible, that Abigail Carmichael is possible.

DEE. Way I see it, we got two options. Stay on the road where we sure 'nough gon' see our

maker and quick. Or, figure on some ways to be the mothers our children deserve and the women we deserve.

SHIFT

RACHEL. Good thing I studied that map like the back of
my hand. Dorothy say's she'll have a few cars to us in
no time. But to stay put in case she needs to call back.

SARAH. ...

RACHEL. Says it's happened before.
All the miles we puttin' in.
Cars, right?
So unpredictable.

SARAH. Whatever you say.

> (*Silence.*)

> (*Silence.*)

RACHEL. How's your sister?

> (*Silence.*)

> (*Silence.*)

SARAH. ...Growing like a stalk that girl.
Never wants to play outside anymore.
*Too much heat, too many mosquitos, everything's
boring.*
That age.

RACHEL. Hmm.
She's working through some things.

SARAH. Sixteen, taller than me and wearing lipstick. Red
lipstick, Rachel.

RACHEL. Good, she likes it.
Sales-girl said it was all the rage.

SARAH. Should've known it was you.

Does she tell you things?
She won't talk to me anymore.

RACHEL. She's an eye-talian lookin' girl in a White family.
What do you expect?

SARAH. I say, Penny, that bra – oh,
yeah! *Penny.*
She doesn't want to be called that anymore.
Penelope.
Penelope, that brassiere is a tad bit small on you. We'll
get you fitted again.
She tells me, I'm wrong.
We – her passive-aggressive word for Black – wear
them *differently.*

RACHEL. Don't take things so personally.

SARAH. That's rich coming from you.

RACHEL. Careful.

SARAH. I'm tired.
Of being careful.
Always.
What will Rachel think if I do this?
Say that?

RACHEL. There are more pressing details to attend to.
An entire country out there needing to be
convinced to trust me, love me, embrace me –

SARAH. Embrace yourself!
How about you start there!

RACHEL. I am <u>not</u> that!
I am not <u>that</u>
Or you! We.
Are different.

SARAH. That what you've been telling Penny?

RACHEL. *Penelope.*

SARAH. Don't you dare chastise me in this very moment.
I asked you a question.

RACHEL. I'd like to know who you imagine you're speaking
to.

SARAH. My cousin, that's who.

RACHEL. I know what we are to each other.
Still doesn't make us more.
Will never make us the same either.
And as for Penelope... She's dodging mosquito bites
and the sun, not because she's sixteen, but to maintain
the porcelain dream she was born into!

SARAH. What is that supposed to mean?

RACHEL. Figure it out.

SARAH. Rachel Helen, you've hurt my feelings.

RACHEL. You're responsible for them, not me.

SARAH. And *you* can't inherit your father's feelings either.
Your father was the one given to the maid to be raised.
Not you.
He was torn away from his sister.
He was the one who grew up calling his parents *Mrs.
and Mr.*
Not you.
And yet, the rest of the family has at least attempted to
reconcile – but not the inculpable Rachel.
You are determined to make us all suffer for something
we can't change.
Our grandmother was young, ambitious and saw an
opportunity
to have a better life so she took it.

You want to crucify her when you have no idea what she endured.
You have no idea the pain and guilt she carries everyday.
Because you won't even speak to her.

RACHEL. *(With disgust.)* Shameful.
Spending her adult life passing for White.
Something she is not.
Yet, my daddy born to a White man – but a bit too dark – gets sent away to live with the Black nanny who got paid to change *your* mother's diapers.

SARAH. I never once said it was right.

RACHEL. Say she was horrific.

SARAH. IT was a horrific time.

RACHEL. That's why we're different.
You can't bring yourself to admit who the real victims are.

SARAH. We can agree the conditions you must endure today are far from perfect.
For her, a high yellow woman sixty years ago?
It took courage.

RACHEL. You echo her perfectly.
Always with the deflection.
Forcing your reaction on another's pain.
Pain you could never begin to comprehend.

SARAH. You're more like her than you care to admit.

RACHEL. Pile on the insults, why don't you.

SARAH. She provided Black women with hope and a blueprint.

RACHEL. All the while impersonating a White woman.
How can I respect that?

SARAH. HOW ELSE COULD SHE INITIATE CHANGE?

HOW ELSE COULD SHE HAVE GIVEN HER FAMILY A NEW BEGINNING?

RACHEL. Same way I'm doing!
Being Negro everyday.
Especially when it hurts!

SARAH. You're both fighting for the same principle.
She, from across the ropes.
What better equipped sister-in-arms than one familiar with the cause.

RACHEL. Oh, don't serve me chitlins and call it caviar.

SARAH. Then swallow this.
It's not that she disassociated herself from her race that upsets you –

RACHEL. Sarah –

SARAH. It's that you didn't –

RACHEL. Stop.

SARAH. Reap any of the benefits!
That's your number and I called it!

RACHEL. ...

SARAH. ....

RACHEL. ...

SARAH. ...

RACHEL. You got to rescue us back there.
Won't for your White
Me, Dee and Abby be breathless right now.
The whole time that man looking past us and at you,
I realized no matter what I said
None of <u>my</u> pretty words would save us.
Dee and Abby knew it too.
That's why we stood there silent.

But I could feel my body reaching for just an ounce of
what you got.
The <u>look</u> of a savior.

> *(Fed up,* **SARAH** *pulls a coin from her purse.)*

Go head.

Call your grandmother if you see fit.
And whatever help she sends,
you take it.

> *(***SARAH*** begins to dial the operator.)*

I'll have no part in her brand of salvation.
Be assured of this.
I don't care <u>how</u> it kills me
I'mma keep going and going and going and going until
something changes.
Because <u>I</u> want to save my people.
I want my people to believe that <u>we</u> can save ourselves
being <u>ourselves</u>.

> *(***SARAH*** hangs up the phone.)*

Your side of the family got the new beginning.
We got thick skin and thin opportunities.
Lackluster futures and dreary pasts.
My father got placed on th*e front* of the ship, on the
back of the bus, on th*e front* line of duty
and the receiving end of discrimination.
Placed there by his own mother.
We got durable bones tested and proven.
We got hell on earth.
Perhaps it be appropriate that I harbor just a tad bit of
bitterness.

> *(***RACHEL*** is preoccupied by her last words.)*

I could use that.

(*Beat.*)

(*Shirley Chisholm-esque voice.*) Not all blood is bleachable
but every heart is reachable.
Every child is teachable.
So the resources shall be equal.
Every woman is capable
therefore her voice shall be audible.
Every person's freedom of speech, love, education, work
and religion shall be... Shall be...
I need to look up a word.
The dictionary's in the car!

> (*A car approaches* **ABBY** *and* **DEE**. *They retreat.*)

DEE. You say Dorothy sent you?

> (*A car approaches* **SARAH** *and* **RACHEL**. *They approach.*)

RACHEL. We sure appreciate you coming this way to find us.

DEE. Okay sistahs.
Well, change of plans.

> (**DEE** *looks at* **ABBY** *who nods in agreement.*)

The two of us
are headed North.

RACHEL. Yes Ma'am that's correct.
We're still heading South.

TRANSITION

(Use this time to introduce the updated world.)

(Project media stories and current events.)

(Use iconic music that incrementally pushes us forward though time.)*

(Until...)

(Present.)

---

* A license to produce *Cadillac Crew* does not include a performance license for any third-party or copyrighted music. Licensees should create an original composition or use music in the public domain. For further information, please see the Music and Third Party Materials Use Note on page iii.

MOVEMENT FIVE

PODCAST VOICEOVER OF SARAH. Support for our podcast, *Uncovering American Herstory,* is brought to you by Bra-less.

The bra so light it feels like you're not wearing one.

And.

By Table 4-1 –.

The food delivery service for singles.

Because sometimes leftovers suck.

For a free trial just go to Table41.com/herstory.

Now

let's start the show.

> *(Recognizable podcast music*.)*

> *(It's important that **SARAH**'s voice and tone echo that of a podcast journalist.)*

JOURNALIST. With improved gender balance in Congress, the House of Representatives,

and our country's first woman Vice President,

is the dawn of a new day truly around the corner?

We take a closer look into the roles of women in revolutionary movements.

Today, we have three prominent Black women activists calling in.

---

* A license to produce *Cadillac Crew* does not include a performance license for any third-party or copyrighted music. Licensees should create an original composition or use music in the public domain. For further information, please see the Music and Third Party Materials Use Note on page iii.

From Public Radio Today, I'm Sarah Brooks and it's [actual day and month].

(*Sounds of protest past and present. Mixed in should be familiar mottos and quotes bellowed out during said protest.*)

(*The introduction of* **PATRISSE**, **OPAL**, *and* **ALICIA** *mimics sound bites – a bit distorted.*)

OPAL. (*Prerecorded.*) Hi, am I speaking with Ms. Smith? If I could share five minutes of your day to discuss the power, we as citizens hold, organize, to galvanize, to mobilize.

(**ALICIA** *in front of a green screen?*)

ALICIA. (*Prerecorded.*) and contribute to the reshaping of our communities and country. Because nothing is more important than exercising our right to build the United States we want to live in.

(**PATRISSE** *streaming live on social media.*)

PATRISSE. (*Prerecorded.*) Wonderful. I was wondering if you'd like to register to vote today?

(*Phones ring.*)

JOURNALIST. Hi, this is Sarah.
Sorry for the technical difficulties, it's always something, but, yeah, yeah, it sounds good now.
I think we're all good.
Do I have everyone now?

ALICIA. I'm here. Hey, ladies, what's up?

OPAL. Here / hey, hey girl.

PATRISSE. Miss ya'll / on. Can you hear me?

JOURNALIST. Yes, great!
I'm recording now.

I'm glad we can finally do this.

Your schedules make it difficult to get all three of you at once.

Do you ever travel as a unit?

PATRISSE. On occasion, we do.

But if we can be three places at once, like now, that's the preferable option.

JOURNALIST. [*Adlib. For example:* yeah, thank God for Zoom, am I right?]

On this podcast,

our singular goal is to uncover the massive and often forgotten or erased legacy of women.

Our episodes usually focus on the past.

So having you three women on the show today is an absolute treat.

In the beginning and for many years to follow, we heard about the movement...but not so much who the catalysts were – are.

Today, your faces and names are widely spread.

But just in case there're still a few folks out there unaware, would you mind introducing yourselves. Where're each of you from?

(Underlayer sound of locations.)

OPAL. Opal Tometi. New York.

PATRISSE. Patrisse Cullors, I'm from Los Angeles.

ALICIA. Oakland based. I'm A-lee-see-ah Garza.

A lot of people think it's Alicia, which has become an awkward icebreaker for engaging folks in person.

JOURNALIST. Okay, so my first question is: How in the world, and for so long, did you maintain such a high level of anonymity? And was that a strategic move on your part?

OPAL. No actually.
It wasn't purposeful.
We've never hidden ourselves behind computer screens
or avoided the media.
It's just that doing the work of organizing
to end all state-sanctioned violence.
That's been priority from the very beginning.

JOURNALIST. The work. How did it start?

PATRISSE. Alicia, go head.
You synthesize this beautifully.

>*(Underlayer of summer sounds: ice cream
>truck, kids playing in the park, etc.)*

ALICIA. I remember it clearly, it was mild weather, a breezy
day, high 60s. July 13th 2013, that was the day Trayvon
Martin was posthumously tried for his own murder.

>*(Sound bite of the Zimmerman decision.)*

So, along with Patrisse and Opal, I got on my computer,
logged into my social media accounts.
I wanted to put my hands around all of us as we cried
millions of tears across the globe, to galvanize our
community in the midst of a very dark time.

>*(Sounds of computer keys clicking away.
>Sounds of internet notifications.)*

It was important to say aloud that we matter.
That our bodies matter.
That we have a right to affirm we matter here...and we
do.
We do.
We always have.

PATRISSE. #BlackLivesMatter.

JOURNALIST. So, Opal, you posted the hashtag on social
media and then what?

(Sounds of a million "Likes.")

OPAL. So simple in words, you know.

Just three: Black Lives Matter.

But it's gigantic to us.

To people whose lives are systematically targeted.

Taken out.

An affirmation provides foundation and meaning to people.

An affirmation can start a war or build a kingdom.

This one, it inflated a community to build a platform of self-love and worth despite the messages society sends.

It went viral.

PATRISSE. People knew it to be true.

Now we're going to proudly make the world acknowledge it.

(Sounds of chants: Black Lives Matter! Black Lives Matter!)

ALICIA. Acknowledge that you believe it or you don't.

If you do, great!

Let's talk.

JOURNALIST. Right, allyship.

ALICIA. Rather, co-conspiratorship.

JOURNALIST. How does one become a co-conspirator?

Specifically

White folks.

How do they function in Black Lives Matter?

ALICIA. To co-conspire is to work together, to mobilize, and move forward toward the same goal

OPAL. Co-conspirators are wonderful and helpful when they actually desire to be change agents.

We're grateful for those people who hear the call, investigate and admit to ways they benefit from the degradation of Black people.
Once we're all there,
we can work together to rebuild the United States.

JOURNALIST. Three Black women –

ALICIA. I'm also queer.

PATRISSE. So am I.

JOURNALIST. And why is that important to name?

ALICIA. We live in a society where Black can often times feel
 synonymous with male and where woman is often
 translated to White. So when you exist beyond those
 ideas you learn the importance of naming and claiming.
 You.
 Our Blackness, queerness and womeness... Is us.
 It's where we are coming from.
 Shapes our particular Black lives.
 And every Black life matters.

PATRISSE. The movement was founded on queer
 feminist framework.

JOURNALIST. So, Black and queer women
 Just the three of you,
 spearhead a campaign that reaches all corners of the
 world,
 sparks massive discussion and debate,
 unites millions
 and facilitates engagement geared towards social
 change in a manner no one has witnessed in decades.
 Maybe since Dr. King and the Civil Rights Movement
 and somehow, it's taken seven years for the world to
 learn your names. To credit you for the work we'd been

attributing to certain men whose platforms and voices were amplified instead of yours.

PATRISSE. Yeah.

JOURNALIST. Surprising?

PATRISSE. No.

OPAL. Men lead, right?

Women have always been in the background championing masculinity, right?

Rhetoric is vital to how we remember history.

This is nothing new.

We've always been here leading, blazing trails.

Most of our society would just rather we stay in the peripheral.

It's more comfortable for people.

JOURNALIST. Why do you think that is, Patrisse?

PATRISSE. Fear. Of equity. Of shifting power. Of change. Of disrupting the status quo designed to serve the interests of a few over those of the masses. When women are on ballots, when queer people, racial minorities or people living with disabilities are on ballots...these identities are centered in the conversations around how efficiently they're able to lead. We recognize this as a fear induced strategy to maintain power. And it has worked for centuries. But people are getting tired –

OPAL. Yup! Of White fragility, male fragility hetero fragility, superseding justice and progress. Folks are radicalizing, hungry for new energy. For improved methods of leadership. And we're seeing more women being voted into civil service duties as a result.

PATRISSE. But this isn't just a result of our work or the work of activists in this generation.

We stand on the shoulders those who've dedicated their lives to fighting the violence this country is founded on. Without our fore-sisters, there is no us. Without a Shirley Chisholm or Barbara Jordan there is no Ayanna Pressley, Ilhan Omar, Alexandria Ocasio-Cortez, Cori Bush. We have to connect the dots and disrupt this country's practice of burying our legacies. Because if we do, we'll always think we're starting at square one when we are not.

Women aren't new to this. We're true to it.

JOURNALIST. You're talking about erasure –

PATRISSSE. Yes...

JOURNALIST. And I'm wondering what role that has played in recognition for the platform you created and work you continue to do. Alicia, can you talk about that a bit?

ALICIA. The theft of Black queer women's work didn't politely pass us by.

We witness it within this movement everyday.

Though I will say it took me by surprise because it came from unexpected places.

Black Lives Matter is a strong, unpalatable statement for some. People feel excluded and uncomfortable.

So they want to change it to include their identities.

All lives matter, Brown lives matter, Women's lives matter, Migrant lives matter...the list goes on and on.

I think that's great.

But when you use the sturdy foundation that Queer Black Women created to catapult your mission but leave them out of the conversation, don't invite them to the table, don't care to entertain their thoughts on how to move forward –

PATRISSE. That's hetero-patriarchy when you ignore us.

ALICIA. Because whether conscious or not, this desire to uplift and take comfort in male/White guidance is historic and strategic.

JOURNALIST. Of course. Do you three ever fear that after it's all said and done, after you've left your heroic stamp on this world, that history books will leave your names absent? That a version of the Black Lives Matter movement will be told without you in it?

PATRISSE. A few years ago, I'd say yes to that question.

ALICIA. We were already being erased. But, today...no.

OPAL. We're more intentional about claiming space. And it's not ego driven.

PATRISSE. Right.
We're just aware of how important precedence was for us
and will be for activists to come.
The dangers of not acknowledging who or what came before
is how stagnation persists.
We have a mandate, and that mandate is to save this country from the jaws of the past, when women, and Black people, and people of color, and immigrants, and queer people, were seen as less than fully human.

OPAL. So then our undertaking becomes two-fold. To do the work of ending state violence while using our resources to document the journey and to name the folks on it.

JOURNALIST. I read on your website that Black Lives Matter has a mandate to claim justice. I'm sure this has to be broken down into steps of some sort. What's the focus at the moment?

OPAL. Great question, Sarah.

JOURNALIST. Thank you.

OPAL. You're welcome.
We're preparing for one of the most significant presidential elections this country has ever faced.

We citizens hold the power and not enough of us take full advantage of that.

Voting is a right. Voting is a duty. Voting is a superpower. Energizing more people to want to take care of this power is what we'll continue to do.

PATRISSE. I think about my mother and the many Black women who've exercised this power…

How they repeatedly vote in the best interest of all people residing in this country.

This is an admission of truth, that for a very long time, Black women have and continue to shoulder the weight of the relentless assault on our people.

Black trans and queer folks fighting to live in a hetero-patriarchal society which refuses to protect us while simultaneously fetishing and profiting off our very existence is an egregious act of state violence.

ALICIA. Let's do our research. Which candidates have an educated and actionable agenda in place to combat these violences? Who has a history of advocating for marginalized communities? And if those candidates don't make the ballot, we still have a duty to vote into office the better of our options. And then we get to work on making it clear what we demand from our elected officials. And holding them accountable to us. You must stand for us. Fight with us or we'll vote you out and find someone who will. That's knowledge we gained from the viral social media spread of the #BLM. News travels faster than ever, people with no financial backing can build platforms and like-minded people will follow.

PATRISSE. Ending this violence is the work.

Silence is violence.

OPAL. We will never be silenced.

JOURNALIST. Every act of violence you just named, Patrisse, the breadth – the scope – it's so large and yet you've taken on the task of ending each of them. How do you fight the exhaustion of it all?

OPAL. We take naps.

PATRISSE. We make art.

ALICIA. We cultivate love and joy and find moments to celebrate as often as we can.

PATRISSE. Exhaustion hits, of course. We're human and very aware that self-care is a part of the task.

But it's our duty to win, we will continue to fight by any means necessary.

(Sound bite of "the deadly stress of being a Black woman in America.")

OPAL. We all get one body, one lifetime to impact the world with our contributions.

Using ours to build a more equitable society is actually energizing.

It's most definitely a legacy worth pursuing.

ALICIA. I found old interviews and letters, some personal, some published of women who've come before us. They offer much insight on legacy, will, and what we've always been up against. Here's one that particularly grabs me.

NEW LOCATION

Past and present

(Lots of weather. Varying weather. The sky cracks and thunder escapes. Lightening bolts. Sun shines in certain spots. Wind bellows. Voices scream, babies cry. People laugh. Protests ensue. Defeat floats. The ground breaks.)

(During this next speech the women embody all the shifts in the atmosphere. Their voices and body movements should match the soundscape.)

PATRISSE/DEE. My sacred America,

I stand before you today as a Negro woman. Some persons need time to gather their prejudices, grip them closely: just from hearing that factual declaration. Please let me warn you to hold on to your hats, in preparation for my next announcement.

I. Am. Proud.

And with such pride comes a responsibility to oneself. A responsibility to one's family, and a responsibility to one's country. This country. My America. Your America. Our stolen land is not by nature a divisive land and I do not intend to contribute to it being so. For we are far more powerful in uniformity than in separatist thoughts and actions. It is when we acknowledge the possessions of our citizen neighbors that indestructible machinery can begin being built. I, the Black American, am your neighbor. He, the Brown American, is your neighbor. The gay Americans are your neighbors. The Americans with disabilities are your neighbors. The American Indian, American Jew, Muslim American, neighbors indeed. She, the less monetarily fortunate American, is your neighbor.

This is not a rebellion. How is it a rebellion to demand access to the rights granted to all citizens of this great country?

This is not a coup.

I have a request of you.

OPAL/ABBY. Please. Close your eyes, rid your conscience of practiced social hierarchy. Now imagine an America where we engage all of our assets, equip our generations equally, shape our children to build towards and not against. An America where hate is a history lesson and love exposes itself in tangible ways. Imagine you. Your dreams, intentions, goals and potential all meeting at the intersection of "Of course I can Avenue" and "My country agrees with me Drive." An America where you are not better than but equal to. An America where we realize the overflowing unified benefit in what equity really means.

JOURNALIST/SARAH. Some of you will reject this. Some will desire a continued life in an egregious America. An America that others bomb, an America where national security is lacking. An America where domestic distrust reigns supreme. It is you citizens that I challenge. I challenge your pride, love and devotion to our great country.

ALICIA/RACHEL. My Sacred America,

There is an entire gender of national heroes ready to champion, protect and grow you. In the form of Black wives, Hispanic mothers, Asian sisters and White daughters who bleed red, white and blue! It is the autonomy that you promised us that we act as neighborly residents, standing side by side with all Americans choosing to respectfully pledge our allegiance.

My sacred America,
When will you be ready for us?

SHIFT

Present

JOURNALIST. Wow.
I find myself posing the same question.
What's the date on that?

ALICIA. 1974. Written decades ago.
By Rachel Helen Christopher.

JOURNALIST. Rachel Helen Christopher?
Who was she?

(*A beat.*)

ALICIA. …
I wish I knew.

End

(*A song reminiscent of "Feelin' Good" by Lauryn Hill*.*)

---

* A license to produce *Cadillac Crew* does not include a performance license for "Feelin' Good." The publisher and author suggest that the licensee contact ASCAP or BMI to ascertain the music publisher and contact such music publisher to license or acquire permission for performance of the song. If a license or permission is unattainable for "Feelin' Good," the licensee may not use the song in *Cadillac Crew* but should create an original composition in a similar style or use a similar song in the public domain. For further information, please see the Music and Third Party Materials Use Note on page iii.